To Ed, forever
E. B.

For Katie, Ben, and Afton
L. C.

First edition 2015

Library of Congress Catalog Card Number 2014939360
ISBN 978-0-7636-6542-5

16 17 18 19 20 CCP 10 9 8 7 6 5

Printed in Shenzhen, Guangdong, China

This book was typeset in Scala.
The illustrations were done in ink and watercolor.

Candlewick Press
99 Dover Street
Somerville, Massachusetts 02144

visit us at www.candlewick.com

Yard Sale

Eve Bunting

illustrated by Lauren Castillo

CANDLEWICK PRESS

ALMOST EVERYTHING WE OWN is spread out in our front yard. It is all for sale. We are moving to a small apartment.

"Small but nice," my mom told me.

She and Dad took me to see it.

He showed me the fun bed that came down from the wall.

"Look," he said. "It's right in the living room."

"It's all nice," I said. But it didn't feel like ours.

Today there are a lot of people walking around our front yard, picking up things, asking the price, though Mom and Dad already put prices on them.

"How much for this?" a woman asks, touching the head-board off my bed.

"Ten dollars," my mom says.

The woman sniffs. "But look, someone has put crayon marks on it. I'll give you five."

My mom sighs. "All right."

I wish I hadn't put the crayon marks on there. They were to show how many times I had read *Goodnight Moon*.

My best friend, Sara, and her little brother, Petey, come over from their house next door. They are both still in their pj's.

"You got a lot of people," Sara says. "That's good."

I nod.

I suddenly see a man loading my bike into the back of his truck.
I rush over to him and grab one of the wheels. I'm really angry.

"You can't take this," I say, pulling on it. "It's mine."

"Oh!" The man looks surprised, but he sets the bike on the
grass. "I'm sorry. I just bought it. Was it not meant to be for sale?"

My dad runs over to us.

"Oh, Callie!" He puts his hand over mine. "We told you, sweetie. We have no place to keep it. And there's no sidewalk outside. Just a street with lots of traffic."

I look up at him, and I think his eyes are all teary. But probably not. My dad doesn't cry.

"It's OK," I say, and I let go of the bike.

"I don't need to take it . . ." the man begins.

"It's OK," I say again. Then I add, "But will you give it back to me when we get our house back?"

The man smiles. "Definitely."

I walk back to Sara.

"I wish you didn't have to go," she mutters. "Why do you, anyway?"

I shrug. "I don't know. It's something to do with money."

Sara picks up Petey's pacifier, which he has dropped, and sticks it back in his mouth before he can scream.

"I don't get it," she says.

"I don't exactly, either."

Sara stares at me. "I could ask my parents if you could stay with us."

I give her a hug. She smells of Froot Loops. "My parents would be lonely," I say.

"Maybe we could give them Petey instead," she offers.

"No offense," I say, "but I'd miss my mom and dad."

"Is this for sale?" a man asks me. He's pointing at a red geranium in a big blue pot.

For a minute I feel important. "I think so," I say. "But you'd better talk to my dad. Over there." I point.

Dad smiles at the man. "It's for sale if you can move it.
It's pretty heavy."

The man rolls it on wheels he's brought and heaves it into
his truck.

Almost everything is gone. Anything that's left my dad is selling cheap. He and my mom look droopy. My dad is rubbing my mom's back.

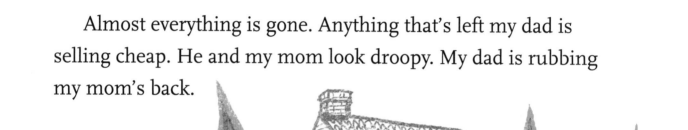

Sara and Petey have gone back to their own house. I hate people buying our stuff. It's not fair. I think I'll give Sara my red heart necklace before we leave. And I'll tell her she can come visit. My mom says.

A woman comes up to me. "Aren't you just the cutest thing?" she says, smiling. "Are you for sale?"

A shiver runs through me, from my toes to my head.

I run to my dad. I'm really bawling.

"I'm not for sale, am I? You wouldn't sell me, would you?"

My dad drops the garden chair he's holding.

"Not for a million, trillion dollars," he says. "Not ever, ever, ever."

He wipes my nose.

Suddenly my mom's there and we are all hugging at once.

Dad stands up and calls out, "Help yourselves to anything that's left. For free. We don't need any of it."

The people who are left scurry around.

We go inside our almost empty house, and it's OK because we don't really need anything we've sold. And those things wouldn't fit in our new place anyway.

But we will fit in our new place.
And we are taking us.
"I think I'll like my new fun bed," I say.
Mom smiles. "I think you will."